LITTLE MISS CHRISTMAS

Roger Hargreaves

Original concept by
Roger Hargreaves

Written and illustrated by
Adam Hargreaves

EGMONT

Little Miss Christmas lives in an igloo at the North Pole, next door to her uncle, Father Christmas, a long, long way from her brother, Mr Christmas.

Little Miss Christmas works for Father Christmas. Her job is wrapping all the presents before Father Christmas delivers them on Christmas Eve.

As you might imagine, there are an awful lot of presents to wrap – it takes her all year long. And as much as Little Miss Christmas loves her job, there are times when wrapping presents day in and day out can get a bit boring.

Last year, after nearly a whole year buried in wrapping paper and sticky tape, Little Miss Christmas decided that she deserved a holiday.

She had nearly finished wrapping all the presents, and thought that it would not do any harm for Father Christmas to wrap the last few himself.

To make it easier for him, she rang her brother at the South Pole and asked him to come and help.

Mr Christmas flew up to the North Pole in his magic, flying teapot on the day Little Miss Christmas left for her holiday.

"I won't be back until the day before Christmas Eve, so you have to make sure you finish wrapping the last of the presents," Little Miss Christmas reminded them just before she boarded her plane.

"Don't worry," boomed Father Christmas. "We've got plenty of time! We'll have them all wrapped long before you return."

The next morning, after a breakfast of Christmas pudding on toast, Father Christmas led Mr Christmas into the wrapping room and they set to work.

"This isn't going to take any time at all," said Father Christmas an hour later. "In fact, we've got plenty of time left. How about a game of golf?"

"Good idea," said Mr Christmas.

And so the two of them played golf for the rest of the day.

The following morning, they settled down to work.
But after an hour, Father Christmas piped up again,
"How do you fancy going reindeer racing?
We've got plenty of time left to do this."

"Good idea," agreed Mr Christmas.

And the two of them spent the rest of the day
racing reindeer across the ice.

The next day, they did not even reach the wrapping room.

"We've still got plenty of time to finish that wrapping. Shall we go fishing today?" suggested Father Christmas at breakfast.

"Good idea," said Mr Christmas, eagerly.

And so it continued.

While Little Miss Christmas lay on a beach in the Christmas Islands (where else?!), blissfully unaware of what was going on, Father Christmas and Mr Christmas were spending a lot of time having fun and very little time wrapping presents.

So you will not be surprised to learn that the wrapping had not been finished by the time Little Miss Christmas returned from her holiday.

"What have you two been doing all this time?" exclaimed Little Miss Christmas, when she saw the huge pile of unwrapped presents.

Father Christmas and Mr Christmas sheepishly studied their feet, unable to look Little Miss Christmas in the eye.

"How are we ever going to get all this done by tomorrow evening?" she continued, angrily.

It was then that she suddenly had an idea.

A brilliant idea.

"We can ask all the Mr Men and Little Misses to help us! And you can go and pick them up in your teapot!" she cried, pointing at Mr Christmas.

By teatime, Mr Christmas had collected as many of the Mr Men and Little Misses as he could find, and brought them to the North Pole.

They all worked right through the night, although Little Miss Christmas had to be careful about which jobs she gave them.

Mr Bump was only allowed to wrap teddy bears because he kept breaking the other presents he was given.

And Little Miss Bossy had to keep a careful eye on Little Miss Naughty, to stop her wrapping nasty surprises in her presents.

Not everything quite went to plan.

Mr Muddle kept writing "Happy Easter" on the labels.

And Little Miss Helpful tried very hard to be helpful, but got into a lot of trouble with the sticky tape.

Mr Forgetful kept forgetting to put presents in his parcels.

And there was no mistaking the presents wrapped by Mr Messy!

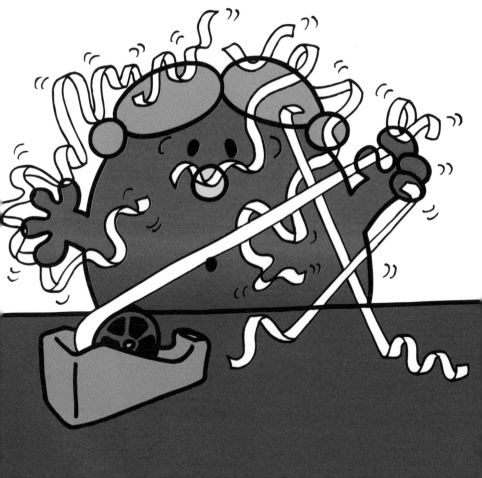

However, by lunch time on Christmas Eve, all the presents were wrapped and labelled and packed away in Father Christmas's sleigh.

"Thank you so much," said Little Miss Christmas to everyone. "I don't know what we would have done without your help. There would have been a lot of empty spaces under a lot of Christmas trees. Now we just need Father Christmas! Has anyone seen him?"

But nobody had.

Eventually, Little Miss Christmas found him playing cards – with Mr Christmas, of course!

"Quick, quick!" she cried. "You're going to be late!"

"Don't worry, don't worry," chuckled Father Christmas.

"We've got plenty of time!"